THE SURGERY BOOK: For Kids

SHIVANI BHATIA MD

ILLUSTRATED BY CHRISTINA GENTH

THE PROCEEDS FROM THE SALE OF THIS BOOK
BENEFIT PEDIATRIC CANCER RESEARCH VIA
Ian's Friends Foundation.

AuthorHouse™
1663 Liberty Drive
Bloomington, IN 47403
www.authorhouse.com
Phone: 1-800-839-8640

First published by AuthorHouse 11/5/2010

ISBN: 978-1-4520-2197-3 (sc)

Library of Congress Control Number: 2010914898

Printed in the United States of America

This book is printed on acid-free paper.

authorHOUSE®

THIS BOOK IS DEDICATED TO MY PATIENTS.
THANK YOU FOR ALLOWING ME THE
PRIVILEGE OF CARING FOR YOU.

SPECIAL THANKS TO DR. SAL GOODWIN FOR TEACHING
ME THE ART OF PEDIATRIC ANESTHESIA.
THANKS TO DOCTOR ANTHONY, AUNT JULIE, SONIA,
& ALL OF MY ESTEEMED COLLEAGUES AT SCOTTISH-
RITE CHILDREN'S HOSPITAL — I AM HUMBLED TO
WORK WITH EACH & EVERY ONE OF YOU.

My name is Iggy. I am a little boy. I have two little brothers – their names are Ziggy and Baby Benji. I also have a doggy named Zoey. I love my brothers (except for when they take my toys).

Ziggy and I share a bedroom. It's pretty cool. We have pictures of cars, construction machines, and fire trucks. Baby Benji has his own room because he cries sometimes and he sleeps in a crib.

My brother Ziggy says that I snore like an elephant at night. Ziggy is only 3 years old, so I don't think he knows what he is talking about. Today, when I woke up I had a runny nose and my throat hurt. I get a lot of sore throats.

Mommy looked in my mouth.
"No school for Iggy today. We need to see a doctor. We need to get you feeling better."

I have the best Mommy in the whole wide world!

Mommy is taking me to see a doctor today for my sore throat. The doctor's name is Doctor Anthony. Mommy says he's really nice. She said he has BIG HUGE tanks full of fishies and LOTS of toys in his office.

I guess I'll go – I do love fishies.

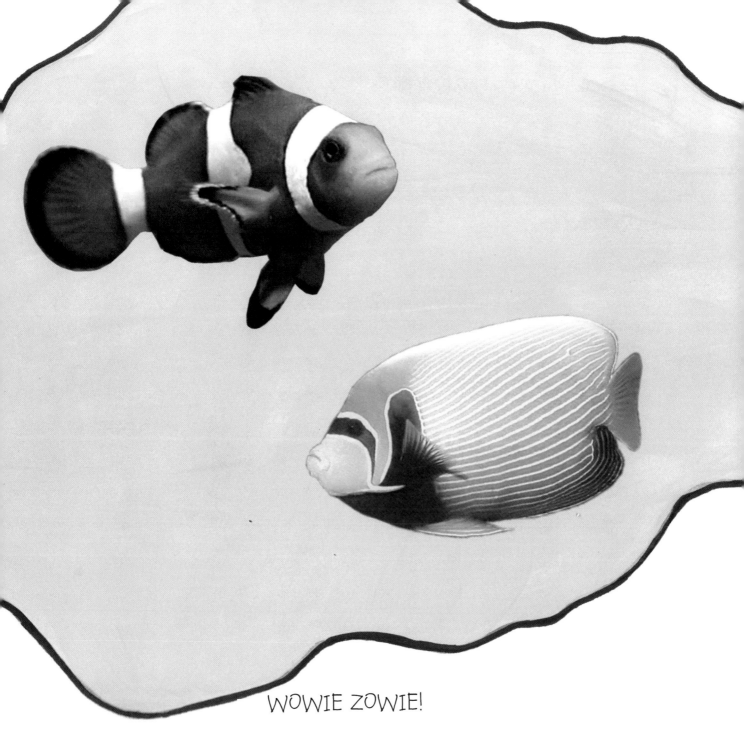

WOWIE ZOWIE!

Doctor Anthony really does have two BIG, HUGE tanks
full of orange and red and blue and purple fishies. He
also has a tank full of jellyfish that change colors!

This place is super cool!

While I watched the jellyfish change colors, Mommy talked to the
lady at the desk. After that we went to a room and waited.

Doctor Anthony came in wearing a funny hat with a mirror on it.
He told me to say "Aaaaaaahhhhhhh," while he looked in my mouth.
He looked in my ears and nose, and then he talked to Mommy.

I like Doctor Anthony, he was nice to me.

"Iggy your tonsils look like GIGANTIC, GINORMOUS marshmallows.
They are the reason that you snore like an elephant when you sleep."

I guess Ziggy was right...maybe I really DO snore like an elephant.

Doctor Anthony is going to take my gigantic marshmallowy tonsils out
tomorrow so that I stop snoring and I stop getting so many sore throats.

Mommy calls Doctor Anthony a sturgeon.

What is a sturgeon????

"It's not sTurgeon Iggy, the word is SURGEON."

Oh, ok Mommy.

A SURGEON IS A SPECIAL DOCTOR THAT CAREFULLY DOES SURGERY TO HELP YOUR BODY AND MAKE IT FEEL BETTER.

A STURGEON IS A TYPE OF FISH!

I am having surgery tomorrow.
What is surgery anyways?

Mommy and Daddy keep saying that word.
What does it mean?

SURGERY IS THE WAY A SPECIAL DOCTOR, CALLED A
SURGEON, LOOKS INTO YOUR BODY AND HELPS IT
FEEL BETTER. SOMETIMES SURGERY IS DONE TO MAKE
SOMETHING STOP HURTING, SOMETIMES IT IS DONE TO
HELP SOMETHING WORK BETTER, AND SOMETIMES IT IS TO
FIX SOMETHING THAT IS BROKEN, LIKE A BROKEN BONE.

So if Doctor Anthony is doing surgery to take
marshmallows out of my throat, won't it hurt?
How will he do that?

I am SCARED.

YOU WILL BE ASLEEP, TAKING A SAFE AND COMFY NAP
DURING YOUR SURGERY. YOU WILL NOT FEEL, HEAR OR SEE
ANYTHING UNTIL YOUR MARSHMALLOWS ARE OUT. YOU WILL
NOT WAKE UP UNTIL SURGERY IS COMPLETELY FINISHED.

"Igs, no eating breakfast before we go to the hospital."

"Daddy, why can't I eat? Ziggy and baby Benji are eating. My tummy is growling really loud like a tiger. I'm super duper hungry."

WE DO NOT EAT BEFORE SURGERY BECAUSE WE WANT OUR TUMMY TO BE EMPTY SO THAT IT IS SAFE FOR US TO FALL ASLEEP.

Here I am! I am at the hospital.
WOW! The fish tanks are so pretty.

Hey, wait a minute, they have toys here? Neat-O!
This place is pretty cool so far.

The people here seem nice, but I still feel scared.

A lady is taking Mommy and Daddy and me to a
room where we are meeting Doctor Anthony.

EVERYONE FEELS SCARED BEFORE SURGERY —
BIG PEOPLE AND LITTLE PEOPLE.
IT IS OK TO FEEL SCARED.

YOU ARE IN A SPECIAL ROOM WHERE YOU WILL
MEET ALL OF THE PEOPLE WHO ARE GOING
TO TAKE EXTRA SPECIAL CARE OF YOU.
MOM AND DAD WILL STAY HERE WITH YOU AND
MEET ALL OF THESE PEOPLE AS WELL.
MEETING THESE NICE DOCTORS AND NURSES
CAN HELP YOU FEEL LESS SCARED.
SOMETIMES THE SLEEP DOCTOR CAN GIVE YOU
MEDICINE TO HELP YOU FEEL LESS SCARED TOO.

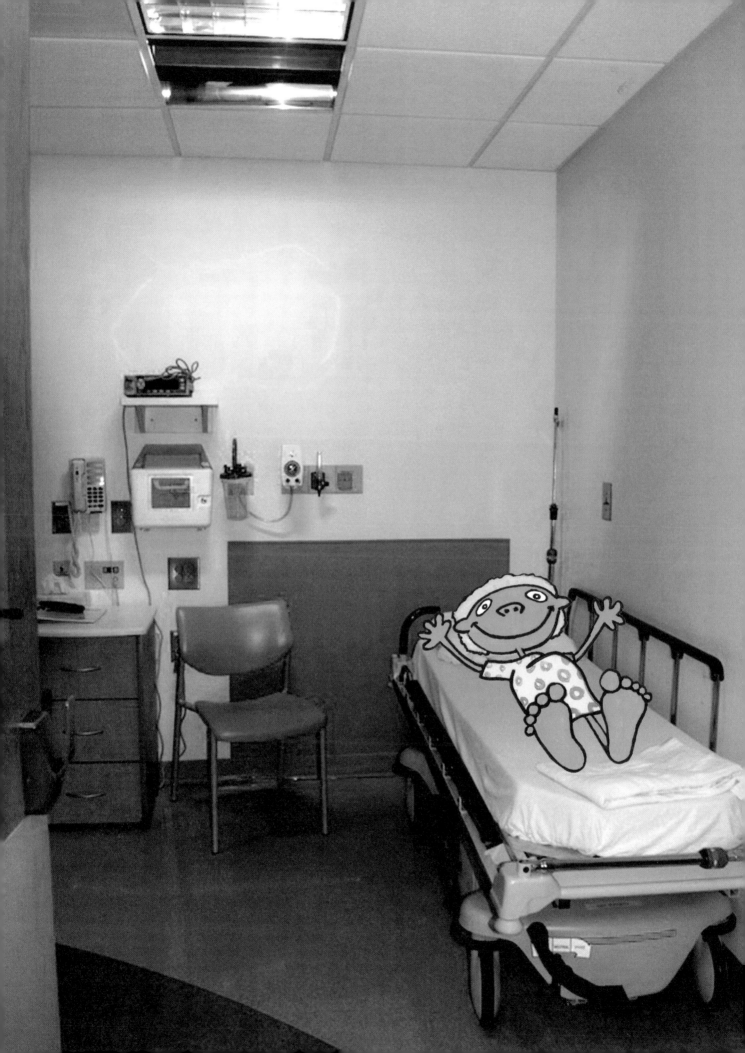

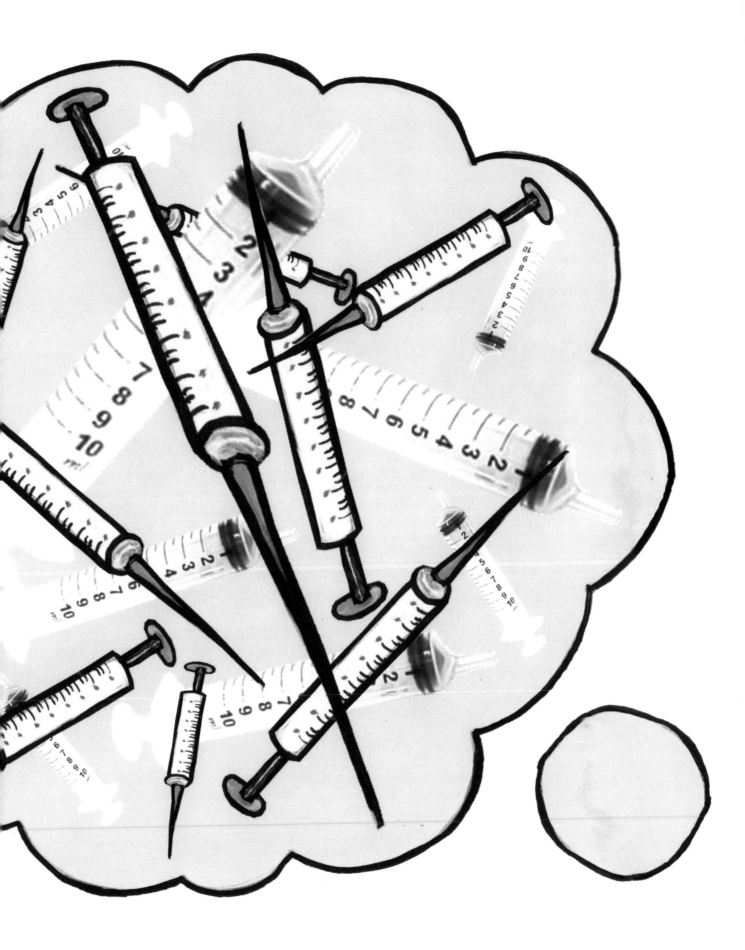

"Iggy, buddy, you are going to be asleep while Doctor Anthony takes your tonsils out and helps your throat feel better."

"But Daddy, I am not sleepy."

THERE IS A SPECIAL KIND OF SLEEP THAT WE
FALL INTO BEFORE WE HAVE SURGERY.
THIS SLEEP IS CALLED ANESTHESIA SLEEP.
DURING THIS SPECIAL SLEEP YOU DO NOT FEEL OR
HEAR OR SEE WHAT IS HAPPENING DURING SURGERY.
IT IS DIFFERENT FROM NIGHTTIME SLEEP.
YOU WILL NOT WAKE UP UNTIL YOUR SURGERY IS ALL DONE.

If I am not sleepy, then how will I fall asleep?

YOU WILL FALL UNDER ANESTHESIA SLEEP WITH
THE HELP OF A SPECIAL DOCTOR CALLED AN
ANESTHESIOLOGIST.
SHE WILL GIVE YOU YOUR SLEEPY MEDICINE.
THIS DOCTOR GIVES YOU SLEEPY MEDICINES EITHER
THROUGH A SPECIAL MASK OR THROUGH A MAGIC STRAW
CALLED AN IV (WHICH STANDS FOR INTRAVENOUS).

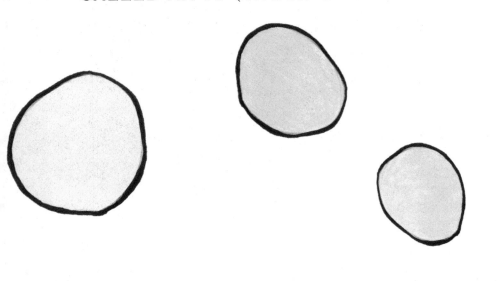

My sleep doctor came and talked with Mommy and Daddy and Me.
Her name is Doctor Shivy.
She wears a funny hat on her head and a blue mask on her face.
She seems nice.

THE SPECIAL DOCTOR THAT HELPS YOU FALL
ASLEEP, STAY ASLEEP, AND STAY SAFE DURING
SURGERY IS CALLED AN ANESTHESIOLOGIST.
YOU WILL GET MEDICINES THAT WILL KEEP
YOU ASLEEP THE WHOLE TIME.
WHEN DOCTOR ANTHONY IS DONE WITH SURGERY,
DOCTOR SHIVY WILL STOP GIVING YOU SLEEPY
MEDICINE AND YOU WILL WAKE UP.
DOCTOR SHIVY ALSO GIVES YOU MEDICINES THAT
HELP YOU NOT TO HURT WHEN YOU WAKE UP.

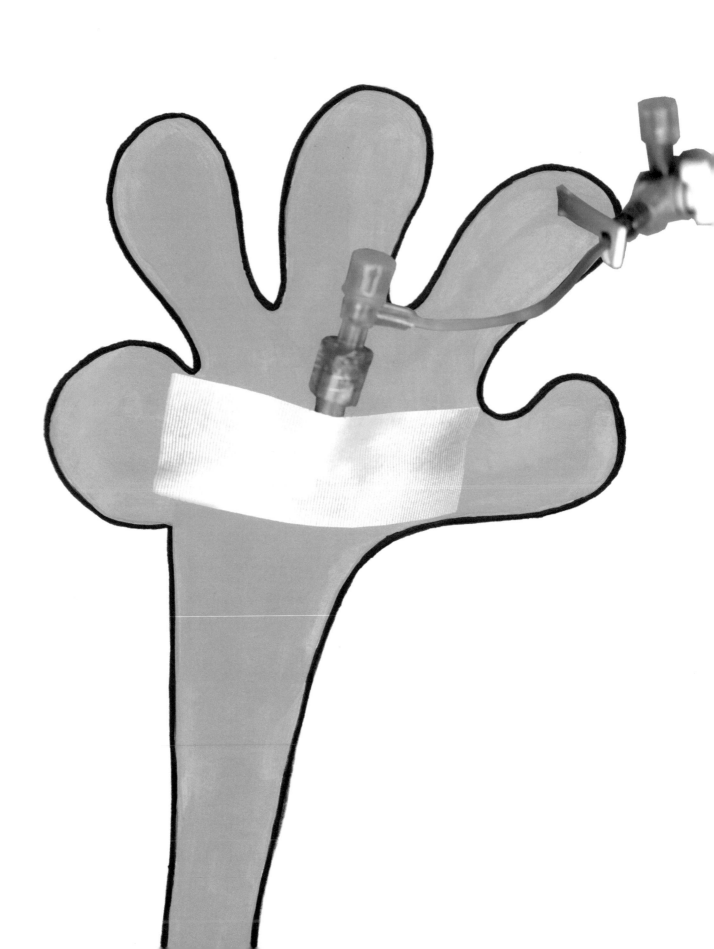

What is an IV straw?
I know what a straw is, but how do I get medicine through it?

AN IV IS A SPECIAL STRAW THAT IS PLACED IN YOUR
HAND, ARM, OR FOOT WHILE YOU ARE SLEEPING.
IT IS CONNECTED TO A BAG OF SPECIAL WATER
THAT HELPS YOU GET SLEEPY MEDICINES AND
OTHER GOOD THINGS YOUR BODY NEEDS.
THIS WATER HELPS KEEP YOU SAFE
AND NOT HURTING DURING THE TIME
YOU ARE AT THE HOSPITAL.

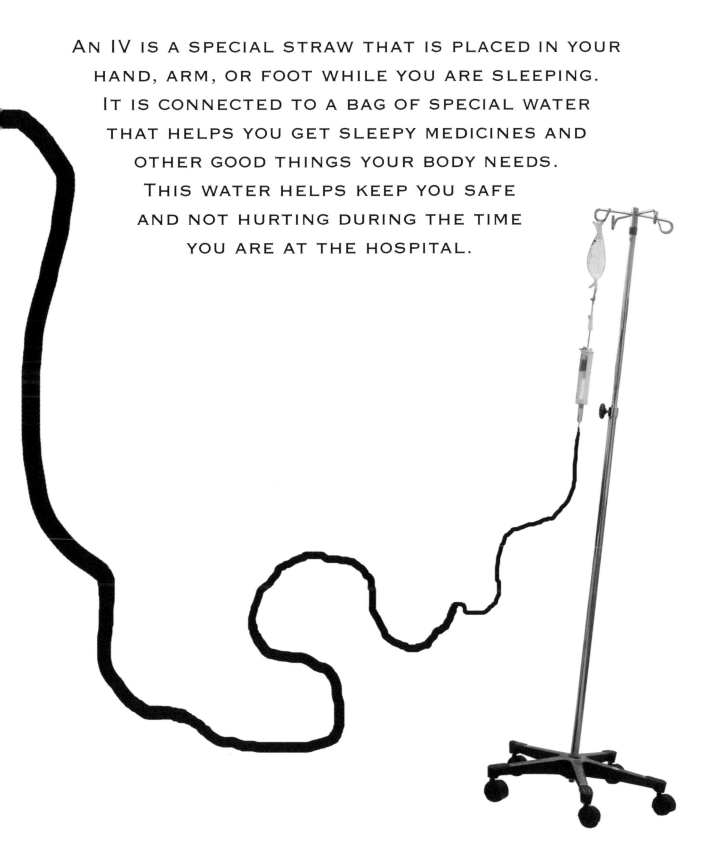

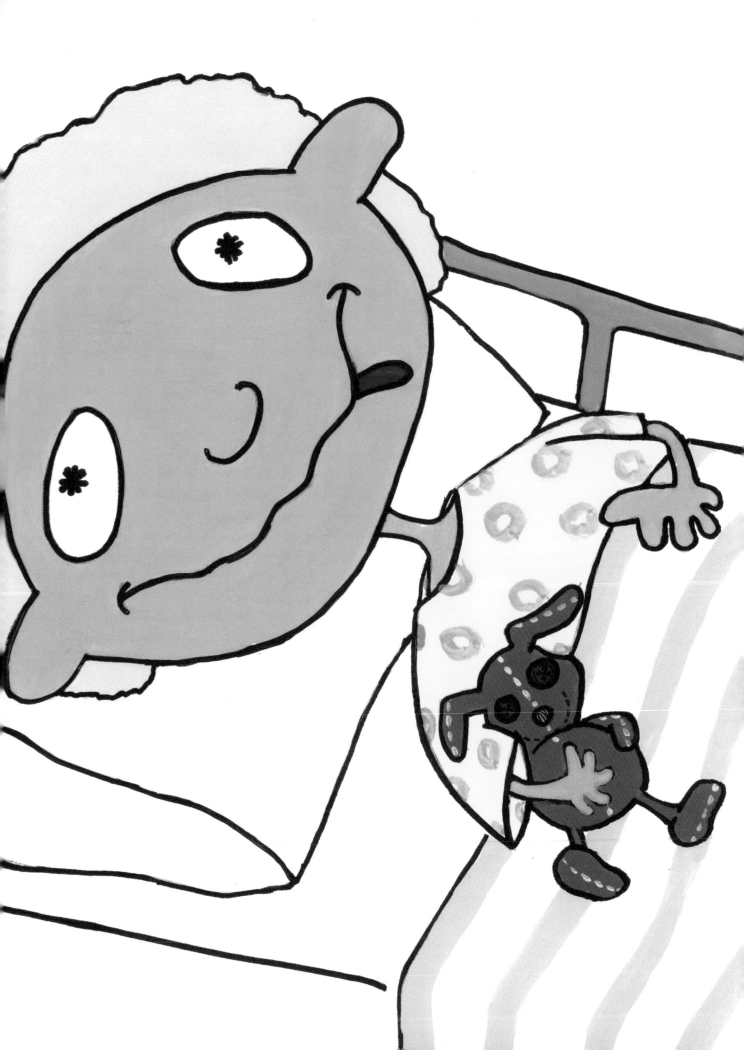

Doctor Shivy gave me some happy juice to drink.

I feel happy...and a little sleepy.

Now I don't feel as scared as when we got here.

HAPPY JUICE IS ONE OF THE MEDICINES SLEEPY DOCTORS CAN GIVE YOU TO HELP YOU FEEL LESS SCARED BEFORE SURGERY.

Nurse Evelyn works with Doctor Shivy and Doctor Anthony.
She is wearing a hat and mask too.

Why?

HATS AND MASKS ARE WORN TO HELP KEEP BAD GERMS OUT.
THE OPERATING ROOM IS SPECIALLY CLEANED FOR
EACH LITTLE BOY OR GIRL THAT COMES FOR SURGERY.
HATS AND MASKS HELP KEEP IT CLEAN FOR YOU.

Nurse Evelyn is taking me back for surgery now. She
is pushing me on a bed with four wheels.

Wheeeeeeee!

I like this!
I feel like a super fast racecar driver!

I am in a different room now. The room is blue and has really big lights that are super bright. It feels cold in here. Brrrrrrrr.

THE ROOM YOU ARE IN IS CALLED THE OPERATING ROOM. THIS IS WHERE YOU WILL HAVE SURGERY (YOUR TONSILS TAKEN OUT) WHILE YOU ARE SLEEPING. YOU MAY SEE BRIGHT LIGHTS, TABLES WITH BLUE TABLECLOTHS, AND PEOPLE WEARING MASKS. ALL OF THESE PEOPLE, TOOLS, AND MACHINES ARE HERE TO HELP TAKE CARE OF YOU.

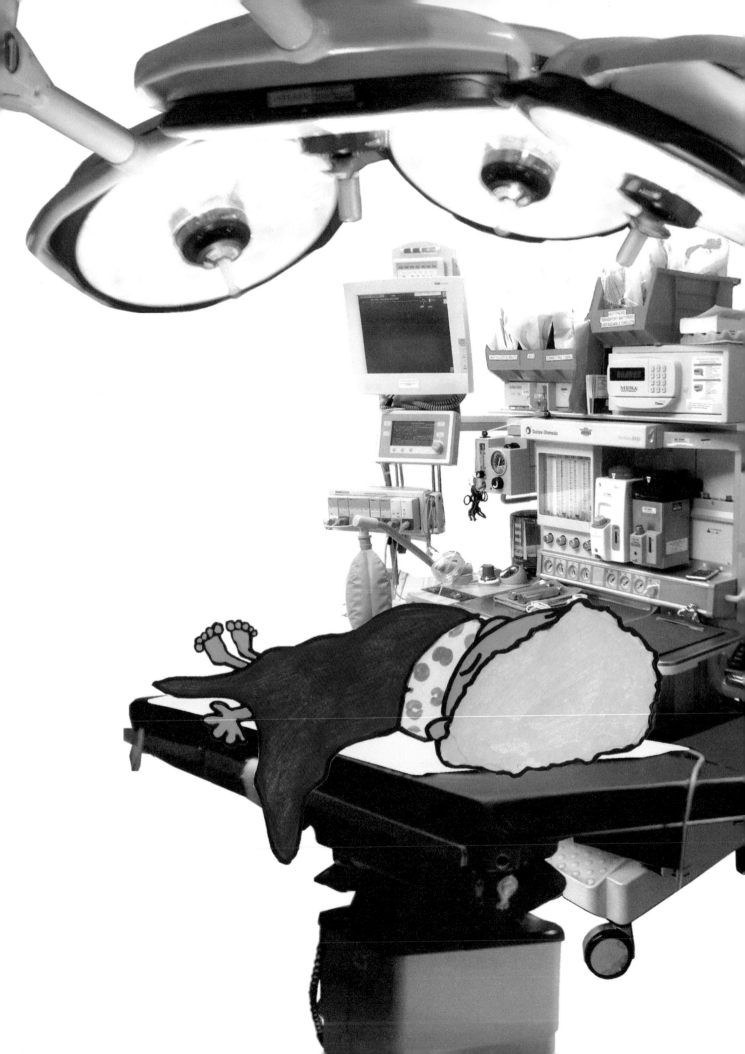

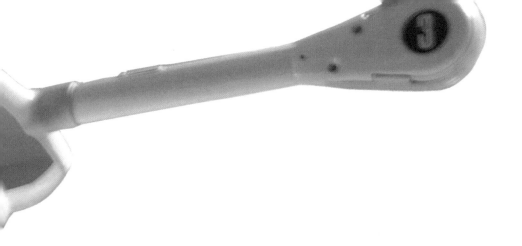

Nurse Evelyn just brought me a super warm blanket. It feels soft and warm, just like when Mommy does laundry. Mmmmmmmmmmmmmm, I feel so cozy now.

Doctor Shivy is putting stickers on me. One on my finger; one...two...three on my heart...and a muscle tester cuff on my arm.

THE STICKERS DOCTOR SHIVY IS PUTTING ON YOU ARE USED TO WATCH YOUR HEART, YOUR BREATHING, AND YOUR BLOOD PRESSURE. THEY HELP HER TO KEEP YOU EXTRA SAFE WHILE YOU ARE SLEEPING.

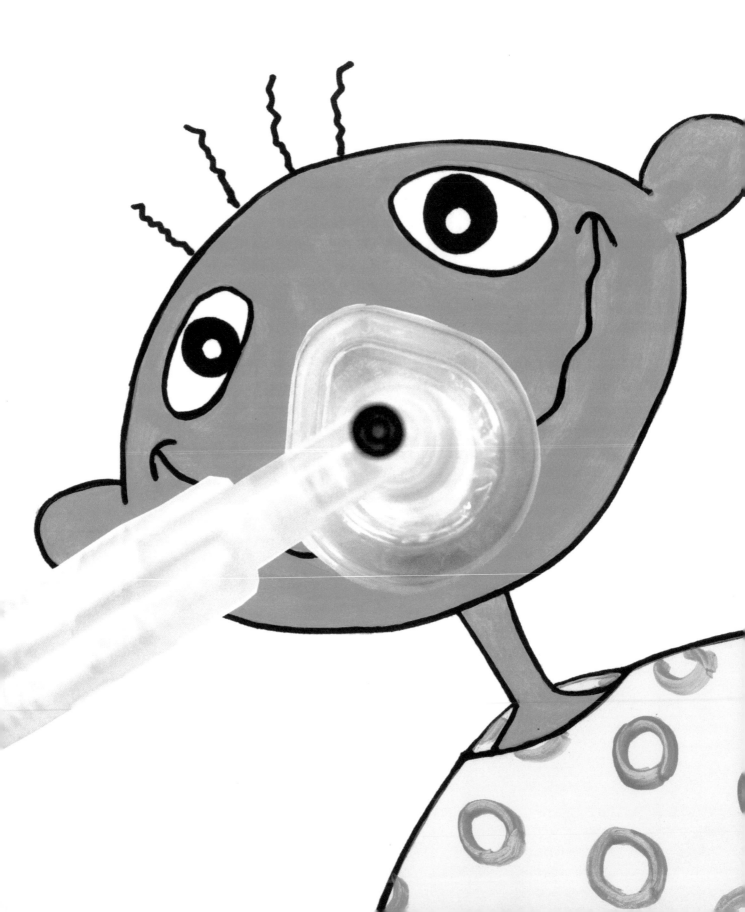

Doctor Shivy is giving me my special mask to breathe through. It smells funny, but it is not stinky. I am laughing...laughing...laughing...

IGGY HAS FALLEN ASLEEP. HE IS WARM, COZY, AND SLEEPING SOUNDLY IN THE OPERATING ROOM. DOCTOR SHIVY WILL STAY WITH HIM THE WHOLE TIME HE IS ASLEEP. IGGY WILL NEVER BE ALONE.

NOW THAT IGGY HAS FALLEN ASLEEP BY BREATHING THROUGH HIS SPECIAL MASK, DOCTOR SHIVY WILL PLACE HIS MAGIC STRAW (IV), AND GIVE HIM MEDICINES THAT WILL HELP HIM FEEL COMFORTABLE AFTER HIS SURGERY. BECAUSE IGGY IS SLEEPING UNDER ANESTHESIA SLEEP, HE WILL NOT FEEL THE IV BEING PLACED IN HIS HAND. WHEN HE WAKES UP HIS IV WILL BE NEATLY TAPED TO HIS HAND. IT IS IMPORTANT THAT HE IS CAREFUL WITH HIS IV AND DOES NOT ACCIDENTLY PULL IT OUT.

"Wake up Iggy. Surgery is over Honey. You are in the wake-up room now" said a sweet voice.

WHAT?
HUH?

Wake up?
Is surgery done?
Are my marshmallows really all gone?
All I remember is drinking some happy juice.
Is that really all?
I thought this surgery thing was going to be super duper scary towns!
It really wasn't so bad.

I do feel sleepy, and it is kind of hard to talk; my throat feels sore.

"My throat hurts."

"Sweetie, let me give you some pain medicine to make it feel better. After a little bit I'll get you a popsicle to eat."

NURSE MISSY GIVES IGGY PAIN MEDICINE IN HIS MAGIC STRAW. IGGY'S THROAT FEELS MUCH BETTER ALREADY.

After a little bit I go back to the room where I left Mommy and Daddy. I eat some popsicles and drink some juice. Nurse Missy talks to Mommy & Daddy for a little while. My throat is feeling a whole lot better.

After I finish my second popsicle, Nurse Missy comes in and says that I get to go home.

YIPEE SKIPPY!!!!!

Nurse Missy gently takes the straw out of my hand. The tape is a little sticky, but it didn't even hurt! I can't believe it!

Mommy helps me put on my clothes.

I am ready to go home now! I'm gonna run super fast so I can press the elevator button.

I guess not – Nurse Missy comes back with a two-wheeled silver and blue buggy for me to ride in! She pushes me in the buggy all the way to our car!

This day has been so super duper amazing, cool and awesome. I can't wait to tell my friends.

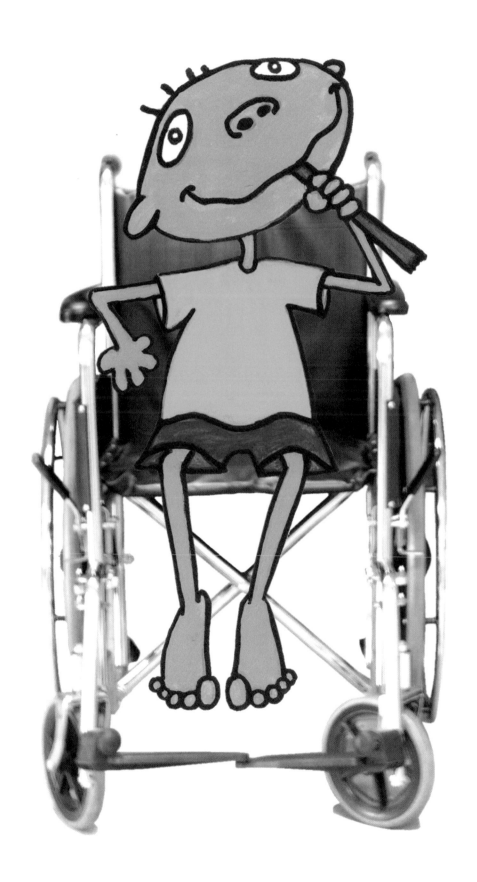

So anyway if you ever have to have surgery it isnt so bad. No shots.

Doctors and nurses are super nice. You get to ride on a bed with wheels and on a 2 wheel buggy. The warm blanket helps you fall asleep. The popsicles are YUMMY.

PLEASE USE THIS PAGE TO DRAW A PICTURE OF
YOURSELF ON THE DAY YOU HAVE SURGERY.
THIS IS A SPECIAL DAY!
YOU ARE GOING TO DO GREAT!

CPSIA information can be obtained
at www.ICGtesting.com
Printed in the USA
LVIC06n1951140218
566539LV00001B/11